D0270877

CAPTAIN VALIANT

And me

REVENGE OF THE BLACK PHANTOM

ADAM BRITTEN
Illustrated by Arthur Hamer

Piccadilly Press • London

This book is dedicated to my wife, Lynn,
without whom the creation of Captain Valiant
would have been impossible.

First published in Great Britain in 2013
by Piccadilly Press Ltd,
5 Castle Road, London NW1 8PR
www.piccadillypress.co.uk

Text copyright © Adam Britten, 2013
Illustrations copyright © Arthur Hamer, 2013

A catalogue record for this book is available
from the British Library

ISBN: 978 1 84812 311 3 (paperback)

3 5 7 9 10 8 6 4

Printed and bound by CPI Group (UK) Ltd, Croydon, CR0 4YY
Cover design by Simon Davis
Cover and interior illustrations by Arthur Hamer

CHAPTER 1

'So, Captain Valiant,' the Black Phantom said, sucking in his stomach and putting his hands on his hips, 'you think you can stop me from destroying London? Well, England's greatest superhero has finally met his match!' He burst into laughter. The Black Phantom did that a lot. It was really annoying. When he laughed he squawked like a parrot. 'Soon the whole world will tremble at my name!'

The Black Phantom dashed up the steps to his laser cannon. He sat in the firing seat and aimed the grey barrel at Big Ben. His hands became a blur as he turned dials and pulled levers.

'Quick, Dynamic Boy,' Captain Valiant shouted, 'we have to stop him before he fires. Turn on the light defractor!'

Captain Valiant picked up a car and threw it at one of the Black Phantom's megadroids. The giant robot turned its huge, square head just in time to see the car coming, but it was too slow to get out of the way.

The car hit it straight between the eyes. There was a roar of purple and yellow flames, and the head shot up into the air like a rocket. Hot metal pinged and pelted the pavement as the megadroid fell to its knees, gears crunching and joints snapping.

It was a good job the streets were deserted. The police and army had kept back the crowds, but the sight of two giant robots and a super villain's secret weapon was enough to make sure there would be someone, somewhere, with a camera. I hoped they stayed out of the way. We didn't have time to save the world and an over-excited tourist!

'Dynamic Boy, I told you to turn on the light defractor.' Captain Valiant flew down and landed in front of me, coughing and spluttering as smoke billowed around him.

'Sorry, Dad,' I said. 'But I didn't bring it. I didn't think we'd need it.'

Captain Valiant shook his head. 'Wait until your mother hears about this.'

'I did bring my screwdriver set.'

I pulled the screwdriver set out of my utility belt, only it was upside down. The lid opened and the screwdrivers fell out. As I bent down to pick them up, an iron claw clamped around Captain Valiant. It was the second 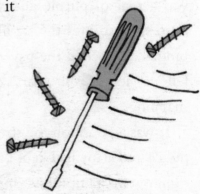 megadroid. It lifted Captain Valiant to its mouth

where rows of saws whirred between its jaws.

'Quick, Dynamic Boy,' Captain Valiant shouted, 'throw me a screwdriver!'

I grabbed the nearest two. 'Crosshead or flathead?' I asked.

'It doesn't really matter.'

I threw the biggest one. Captain Valiant caught the screwdriver and hurled it inside the megadroid's mouth. The giant robot stopped moving. The saws stopped whirring. There was a low rumble, like a burp. A stinking, yellow gas hissed out of the megadroid's backside and the robot fell on its face. Captain Valiant pulled himself free.

'Right, now for the laser cannon,' he said.

Big Ben started to chime. The Black Phantom's laugh echoed across the street.

'You're too late, Captain Valiant,' he cried. 'My megadroids have delayed you long enough. Tonight, London dies!'

The laser cannon hummed. It rose from the ground on a metal platform which rattled and groaned. Its grey barrel sparked like a firework.

'I have no choice, Dynamic Boy,' Captain Valiant said. 'I'll have to absorb the blast!'

'But you know what happened the last time you did that,' I said. 'You had an upset stomach for a week.'

'It's a small price to pay to save the world.'

'Not when we only have one bathroom, it isn't.'

I ran across the street, leaping over the fallen

megadroids. The humming from the laser cannon grew louder. I dashed under the platform, jumping over cables and wires. The cannon whined. There was a

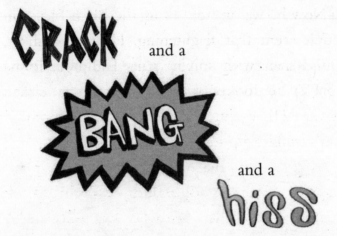

CRACK and a BANG and a hiss

The Black Phantom shrieked with laughter. Then everything went quiet.

'Well done, Dynamic Boy,' Captain Valiant said, hovering over the laser cannon. 'What did you do – block the particle flow?'

'No,' I said. 'I took this out.' I held up an electric plug.

The Black Phantom saw the plug, shouted something *very* rude and continued to turn dials and pull levers. Captain Valiant soon stopped him. He flew to the cannon, dragged him out of his seat and brought him down to earth with a thud.

Now he was in front of us, the Black Phantom didn't seem that frightening. He was a short, round man with stubby arms and legs. To be honest, he looked like an overgrown garden gnome. His costume didn't even fit properly. It had wrinkles around the neck and ankles.

'Right, now that we've foiled your plan,' Captain Valiant said, pulling off the Black Phantom's mask, 'let's see who you really are.' A fat face with small eyes and a twisted mouth stared back at us. 'Well, well, Dr Simon Kirby. So this is what you were doing with the government's money. Rather than developing a form of renewable energy, you made a laser cannon.'

'And I would have got away with it as well, if it wasn't for you pesky superheroes,' Kirby sneered. 'For years I've worked in secret, following orders, doing what I was told. But I should be the one giving orders. I'm the genius – ME, the Black Phantom, the greatest criminal mastermind of them all!'

Captain Valiant pointed at the plug. 'If you're such a genius, why did you use a plug?'

Kirby shrugged. 'You should have seen the size of the battery. It was as big as a house.'

I sighed and threw the plug down. I was tired. It had been a long night. I had better things to do than listen to another super villain going on about why he should take over the world.

'Look, Dad, if we're finished here, can we go home now? I have a maths test in the morning.'

Kirby laughed and raised a stubby finger. 'The only test you have coming, Dynamic Boy, is the test of doom!'

Captain Valiant and I looked at each other. We didn't know whether to laugh or take him seriously.

'What's that supposed to mean?' I asked.

Kirby laughed until his face wobbled and little, greasy tears dribbled down his cheeks. 'You'll find out soon enough,' he said. 'It's coming, Dynamic Boy, the test of doom!'

CHAPTER 2

We got home at midnight. All I wanted to do was go to bed. I left Dad in the kitchen. He always got hungry after a fight. I went to my room, undressed and hung my costume up in the secret compartment behind my wardrobe.

Before I closed the door, I took a long look at my costume. To be honest, I didn't like it. Dad got the red, white and blue jumpsuit. Mum got the red, white and blue cape and tights. My sister got the cloak of invisibility. All I had was a black and gold thing with a lightning flash down the front. I looked like an electric bee.

And what about my name, Dynamic Boy? Now, Captain Valiant, that was fine. Ms Victory, that suited Mum. Moon Girl, that was a good one, even though it was my sister's. But Dynamic Boy? I wanted to be like one of the American superheroes. They had much better names. Thankfully, we lived in England. The English weren't bothered about what superheroes were called as long as it was spelt properly.

I climbed into bed. I heard Dad clattering about with the frying pan, making a bacon sandwich.

Mum didn't like us eating Earth food. She said Earth food was full of fat, sugar and salt. Astral

Guardians shouldn't eat too much fat, sugar and salt. Dad said that since we were living on Earth, we should be like everyone else, even if that meant putting on a bit of weight. Dad liked bacon sandwiches a lot.

Back on our home world, it was against the law to eat meat. I think  that's the only reason Dad joined the Astral Guardians. Being part of an intergalactic police force meant that you were supposed to blend in with the beings on your assigned planet. Dad said that protecting the Earth from alien invasion and super villains meant making sacrifices, and his sacrifice was eating bacon sandwiches.

My sacrifice was a stupid name and a silly costume. It was also having to put up with a sister who wore her cloak of invisibility around the house.

She appeared at the end of my bed. Off came the hood and there was Emma, glistening in the light-absorbing material that turned her invisible.

'Well, how did the fight with the Black Phantom go?' she asked.

'Go away,' I replied. 'I'm tired and I have a maths test in the morning.'

'Don't get moody with me. I only wanted to make sure you were all right.'

I sat up and stared at her. Sometimes, being able to create illusions had its advantages. I turned Emma into a huge slug.

'You look really good covered in slime,' I said.

A pair of dirty socks landed on my head. 'Next time it'll be something heavier,' she said.

I threw the socks at the slug. All right, so maybe creating illusions wasn't much of a superpower. It wasn't fair. Dad could fly and had super-strength.

Mum was super-fast and super-clever. Emma could become invisible and move objects with her mind. All I could do was fly and create illusions. But no one cared about illusions. All people wanted to see were big fights and big explosions. The only reason people noticed me was because of that stupid costume. They even got my name wrong most of the time!

'Why don't you —' I said, but there was a knock on the door. The slug vanished. The door opened and Dad stood there in his pyjamas eating a bacon sandwich. He didn't put the light on. He looked round the room and said, 'Bed.'

I don't know how he saw it but, as Emma passed, Dad took the cloak of invisibility off her. She stood in her pink nightshirt, looking very sorry for herself.

'I've told you before,' he said, 'no superpowers in the house. At home, we try to be like a normal family.'

'Sorry,' Emma replied, and went to her room.

After swallowing the last of his bacon sandwich, Dad turned to me.

'You did a good job tonight,' he said.

I pulled the duvet up to my chin and said nothing.

'What's wrong?' he asked.

'Nothing,' I replied.

'Nothing?'

'Nothing.'

I felt Dad's eyes on me. I thought he was going to say something. He didn't. The door closed. I stared at my bedside alarm and watched the green numbers change. It was quarter past twelve. I was going to be so tired at school in the morning.

The Black Phantom was right. The maths test really would turn out to be the test of doom. I was going to fail it badly. Not even superpowers could save me from the headteacher's detention.

CHAPTER 3

But I was lucky: I didn't have a maths test. When I got to school, it had been cancelled. This probably had something to do with the fact that the school had disappeared. All that was left was a very big hole.

I always walk to school on my own. Dad said I should go with Emma but I usually found an excuse not to. Emma didn't mind. She was a year older than me and said that I embarrassed her.

Besides, walking to school on my own gave me time to think.

It was hard being an Astral Guardian. Don't get me wrong. I may not have liked my costume or the name 'Dynamic Boy', but I enjoyed the superhero bit. I just wished I was better at it. I also liked living on Earth: the weather wasn't bad, the food was good and the people were friendly. We'd been here for just over a year, so I already thought of the place as home. What was difficult was trying not to be different.

When they weren't Captain Valiant and Ms Victory, Mum and Dad were Robert and Louise Taylor, IT Consultants. They stayed at home all day, running a software business. They had no idea what it was like trying to be the same as Earth children. Thankfully, we had been sent to a planet with lots of its own superheroes. In the classroom no one really talked about them. There's nothing special about super-strength or super-speed when someone, somewhere, is always crawling up walls or flying around in a metal suit or shooting beams out of their eyes.

But what did I say when someone wanted to talk about what I did last night? I couldn't tell them the truth. I had to say that I stayed in and did my homework. It would have made things much easier if  we had a secret base. Superheroes shouldn't live in a house or go to school. We should be super all the time. At least then I wouldn't have to sound like a nerd in the classroom.

That's why I was glad the school had disappeared. It was going to be a nerd-free day.

When I arrived, a line of brightly coloured coats and bags stretched down one side of the road and, darting in and out of them, I saw the grey figures of teachers. Cold faces were pressed against the school fence as parents parked or pulled up in the middle of the road to stare at the empty space where the school had been. A police car had mounted the pavement and an officer was on the radio.

'Mark,' I heard above the crowd. 'Mark!'

It was David. He pushed his way towards me. As usual, he didn't watch what he was doing and his bag smacked a couple of Year 10s in the face. They gave him dirty looks and one of them threw a punch which missed.

David was one of the few people who treated me like a friend. I don't know why. I was too secretive and quiet. This didn't bother David. He was small and thin with freckles and ginger hair. He also had a scar down the side of his face. I didn't know how he got the scar and I never asked. David, like me, had secrets.

'The school, it's gone,' he said. 'Look, it's not there.'

He grabbed my arm and pulled me towards the fence. We stood on a bank which ran along the edge of the playing fields. On a normal day you had a good view of the school from this point.

'It's certainly a big hole,' I said.

'Big? It's huge! Do you think the school fell in it?'

'No.'

'Why not?'

'Because there are no bricks or broken glass or anything. If the school had fallen in there'd be something left.'

David put his head against the railings and stared. 'Maybe it's a really deep hole,' he said.

'Is that Mr Stephenson by the gates?' I said. 'Let's go down and see what's happening.' By the time we reached our headteacher, more police had turned up. They were directing parents away from the school. A fire engine had arrived and couldn't get up the road because of the parked cars. Mr Stephenson was talking to Mrs Crowley and Mr Turner. All three had serious faces. The headteacher and his deputies were very serious people. Mr Collins, the caretaker, joined them.

'I've asked around,' Mr Collins said, 'but no one seems to know anything. They all say the same thing. It was here last night and now it isn't. No one heard anything and no one saw anything. The school just vanished.'

'A school can't just vanish,' Mr Stephenson said. 'Someone must have seen something.' He looked as if he was about to lose his temper. Mr Stephenson liked to shout a lot.

'I think we can rule out robbery,' Mr Turner joked.

Everyone ignored him.

'Isn't there an old mine under the school?' Mrs Crowley said. 'Maybe it collapsed.'

Everyone ignored her. Mr Collins coughed as if he had something important to say.

'What?' Mr Stephenson asked.

'The last teacher to leave yesterday was Mr Kirby. I locked the school gates behind him. Maybe he saw something.'

'Where is he?'

'I'll see if I can find him,' Mr Turner said.

Mrs Crowley put her hand on Mr Stephenson's arm. 'Don't worry, Andrew,' she said. 'Everything will be fine.'

'Deirdre, a thirty million pound school has just disappeared. I think we can assume everything will not be fine. In fact, I have every suspicion that things are going to get a lot worse!' Mr Stephenson pointed up into the sky where a familiar red, white and blue figure hovered. 'If there's one thing I don't need at the moment, it's Captain Valiant. When a superhero turns up, you know there's going to be trouble.'

'Well, at least he's on his own,' Mrs Crowley said. 'He doesn't have Ms Victory, Moon Girl or Dynamite Boy with him.'

'Dynamic Boy,' Mr Stephenson corrected.

'Really? Is that his name? I thought it was Dynamite. Oh well, it's a silly name. And have you seen his costume? It's awful. He really should try to get something in red, white and blue. Captain Valiant looks so handsome.'

CHAPTER 4

I tried not to look too interested when Dad landed. It wasn't difficult. Most of the crowd seemed more interested in the hole. There were a few people who pushed their way through to get a better view of him. They were mostly women. Like Mrs Crowley, they probably thought that a man in a red, white and blue costume looked handsome, even when that costume was too tight. Dad really had to cut out those bacon sandwiches.

'So, what's happened here?' Captain Valiant asked as he stood next to Mr Stephenson. 'Is anyone hurt?'

'Nice of you to call by,' Mr Stephenson said. 'Were you flying past or are you on your way to save the world again?'

'No, sir. I was monitoring the police radio and . . .' Captain Valiant pushed open the school gates. There was a sharp crack. Mr Stephenson shook his head. 'Please, Captain Valiant, the only thing I have left of the school is the fence, the playing fields and he gates. I know you're trying to help but you've just broken the gates.'

Captain Valiant didn't seem to hear Mr Stephenson. He walked through the gates, crossed the square of tarmac which had been the car park, and stood on the edge of the hole. He stared into it, jumped up and down, looked back at Mr Stephenson, went to speak and then disappeared. The ground had given way under him.

'So now we have to rescue a superhero,' Mr Stephenson said.

Captain Valiant flew out of the hole and landed back at the school gates. He was covered in mud. It dripped off his nose and trickled down his

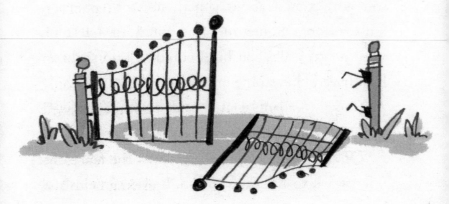

stomach. There was a metal box under his arm. It looked like a microwave oven.

'Going into the catering business?' Mr Stephenson asked.

'No, sir. I found this at the bottom of the hole. I suppose it must belong to the school. With your permission, I'd like to have a closer look at it.'

'Do whatever you like,' Mr Stephenson said. 'I have more important things to worry about than a microwave oven.'

Captain Valiant thanked him, wiped mud from his face and was about to fly off when a voice shouted, 'Captain Valiant!'

It was David. He was one of those people who still got excited about superheroes. It was very embarrassing. Sometimes I wanted to tell him what it was really like, but I couldn't. I don't think he'd have believed me anyway.

'Captain Valiant,' David said, pushing through the crowd. 'Can I have your autograph, please?'

'Of course.' Captain Valiant handed the microwave to Mr Stephenson. It was obviously a

lot heavier than Mr Stephenson expected. He fell
backwards under the weight. 'What's your name,
young man?'

'David Smith, sir.'

David gave Captain Valiant an exercise book
and a pen. Captain Valiant wrote on the book.

'I think you're brilliant,' David said. 'I wish I was
a superhero.'

'Well, perhaps you will be one day.' Captain Valiant ruffled David's hair. 'Everyone can be a hero if they work hard and do their best.'

'Really?' David said.

'Of course. You don't need a costume and superpowers to change the world. Now, if you'll stand back, young man . . .'

Captain Valiant looked around for Mr Stephenson, saw him on the ground, lifted the microwave off his chest, helped him to his feet and flew off.

David watched him, wide-eyed and open-mouthed.

Mr Stephenson watched him and swore under his breath.

CHAPTER 5

I didn't stay at school long after that. I wanted to know what Dad found so interesting about a microwave oven. But I had a problem: David had that I-don't-know-what-to-do look on his face.

'Where are you going?' he said as I walked away from the school gates.

'Home,' I said.

'Right. I thought . . . well, I thought we could hang around here for a bit.'

'Why?'

'I don't know. Perhaps we could . . . no, it doesn't matter.' David turned away.

Like I said, it wasn't easy for me to make friends. I had too many secrets. I left David on his own and walked home.

The house was empty when I got in. Mum and Dad were probably in the laboratory; that's where Dad would have taken the microwave and that's where Mum would be working on it.

The laboratory was under the house. It was hidden behind a secret panel in the floor of the utility room. If you turned the washing machine dial to eco-wash and pushed in the pre-rinse and quick spin buttons at the same time, the machine slid to one side to reveal a flight of steps. At the bottom of the steps, a steel door opened into a short corridor which led to the laboratory. It was a square, white room full of machines which beeped and pinged. There were screens which showed squiggly lines and columns of scrolling numbers. Wherever you looked there was always a red, yellow or green light flashing.

'Hello, Mark, you're home early,' Mum said. 'Is the school closed today?'

Mum had a sense of humour which wasn't funny. She stood in front of a containment chamber. There were four of them set into the wall opposite the door. They were like giant test tubes which went from the floor to the ceiling. Anything which needed analysing went into a containment chamber; that's where all the technical stuff happened.

They were also used to make sure we stayed healthy. Once a week, Mum made us get in and have a check up. Dad often complained that the settings on his chamber were wrong. The results usually showed that he needed to lose weight.

But Dad had other things to worry about today. He stood next to Mum in his Captain Valiant costume. His mask lay on top of a computer, next to a plate with breadcrumbs on it. He'd probably made himself a bacon sandwich while Mum brought the microwave to the lab.

Mum went to a computer and tapped at a keyboard. The containment chamber hummed. The microwave was inside the chamber.

'Are those readings accurate?' Dad asked, pointing at a monitor.

Mum nodded.

'That's the second time you've asked and the third time I've checked. There's no doubt about it, this microwave is a gravity engine.'

'What's a gravity engine?' I asked.

'It's an energy source,' Mum replied. 'It's what

makes intergalactic flight possible. A gravity engine folds space and time so that you can travel anywhere, over any distance, and arrive at exactly the moment you left. At least, that's what it's supposed to do. This one hasn't been built properly. It's misfired. That's why your school has disappeared.' Mum tapped at the keyboard again.

'This engine doesn't fold space and time, it blows a hole right through them. Your school has been blasted across the universe.'

'Perhaps that's what they mean by further education,' I said.

'Mark, this is serious. You can't go around ripping holes in space and time. We're lucky we still have the microwave. Something must have gone wrong with the proton field – that's why your school fell through the hole and the microwave didn't. But if the microwave is still here, it means anything could have come through the hole before it collapsed.'

Dad frowned and pulled at his costume where it was tight across his stomach.

'So this is a kind of energy source?' he said.

'Yes,' Mum replied.

'The kind of energy source which, if it worked properly, could solve most of the world's energy problems?'

'In theory. But it's very crude. It would need a lot of work.'

'But it's the sort of thing Dr Simon Kirby might have been working on?'

The Black Phantom! I remembered what he'd said about the test of doom. If this was it, I really would have preferred a maths test.

Mum picked up a piece of paper. 'That's exactly what I thought. This is the address. I found it on

the electoral register. There aren't any recent photos, so you better take Mark with you to make sure you get the right man. Kirby doesn't have a Facebook page, a website or a blog.'

'But why are we going after the Black Phantom?' I asked. 'We've already caught him and handed him over to the police.'

Dad picked up his mask and pulled it over his head. As usual, he put it in on back to front and had to pull it round so that he could see. 'We're not going after the Black Phantom,' he replied. 'We're going after his brother, *Andrew* Kirby.'

It took me a moment to work out who Dad meant.

'You mean Mr Kirby? The head of science at my school? He couldn't build a gravity engine.

He's too old and boring. He doesn't even know how to use a photocopier.'

'That doesn't change the fact that his brother is the Black Phantom,' Mum said. 'It's too much of a coincidence. Your school disappeared on the same night as the Black Phantom tried to destroy London. It's possible Andrew Kirby knows something about it or is involved in some way.'

'That's silly,' I replied. 'You don't get families of super villains.'

'Why not?' Mum frowned. 'You get families of superheroes.' She tapped at the keyboard again. The microwave disappeared. That was the other thing a containment chamber did: it got rid of dangerous stuff. 'Now, Mark, go and get changed. You might have the day off school, but you still have work to do.'

CHAPTER 6

You'd think, wouldn't you, that when I had to change into my costume it would mean doing something a bit more spectacular than going to my room. You'd expect a flash of lightning or a crack of thunder. Then . . .

. . . schoolboy Mark Taylor would turn into Dynamic Boy. Well, that didn't happen to me. When Mum told me to get changed, I went upstairs, undressed, went to the toilet (you never know when you'll get another chance to go), put on my costume and went back to the laboratory.

Mum checked me over. She straightened my

mask and made sure it was on properly. 'Now, have you been to the toilet?' she asked.

'Yes, Mum.'

'And have you put your clothes away? I don't want to find your room in a mess when I go upstairs.'

'Yes, Mum.'

'And have you changed your underwear? You know it's always better to wear a clean pair of pants when flying.'

'Yes, Mum.'

She pressed a button on the console next to her. A containment chamber slid open and a particle web appeared inside. It glowed, big and green, as if someone had sneezed and left a huge bogey floating in mid-air.

I didn't like using the particle web. It made me feel sick. But it was probably the most important gadget the Astral Guardians had. It was an energy field which could be used for just about anything. Mum had tried to tell me how it worked, but when she got all technical, I got very bored.

All I knew was that it did something with atoms. I asked Mum if it was like a matter transportation beam. She told me not to be silly. Matter transportation beams were science fiction. The particle web was science fact.

Whatever it was, the particle web was very good at getting you to places quickly. We used it to get around the world – it was faster than flying. But it could do much more than that. When we had our weekly health check, the particle web

scanned us and, if there was anything wrong, Mum used it to put us right.

Unfortunately, it didn't stop Dad eating too many bacon sandwiches; that's why he still had a weight problem. Mum said the particle web wasn't there to make us lazy. It was no excuse for not eating a healthy diet.

'Now, you promise to be careful,' she said.

'I'm an Astral Guardian, Mum. I don't do careful.'

'You know what I mean.'

'All right, I promise not to talk to strangers or get into fights.'

'Just promise not to do anything silly.'

Mum gave me her usual kiss on the cheek and I stepped into the containment chamber. The door slid shut and the web surrounded me. I saw nothing but a green glow and tiny, flashing lights. Then I found myself on a roof.

It was windy and cold. Opposite me there was a pigeon perched on the edge of a chimney. For a moment, we stared at each other. Then there was a loud crack and I fell. When the dust cleared, I lay on a wooden floor, staring up through a jagged hole at a very unimpressed bird.

Captain Valiant's face appeared at the hole. 'I expected you to fly,' he said, landing beside me. 'Did you think we were going to knock on the front door?' He pointed over my shoulder. 'That's Mr Kirby's house. His attic is through that wall.'

'There's nothing wrong with knocking on the front door,' I said. 'At least it might have been quieter than falling through the roof.'

'Don't worry. This house is empty. We're not going to disturb anyone.'

I looked round. Dad was right. There were cobwebs everywhere. The only thing that lived here were spiders.

He walked across to the wall and raised his fist. 'Knock, knock,' he said.

When Captain Valiant punched the wall I expected to hear the crash of brick. Instead, I heard a loud, echoing boom. The wall seemed to be made of metal. Captain Valiant winced, rubbed his knuckles and punched the wall again. This time it cracked. There was a hiss and a high-pitched whine. A flickering, silver light shone through the crack.

'I don't think I should have done that,' he said.

Before I knew what happened, Captain Valiant grabbed me and shot through the roof. As we sped upwards, there was a flash and a roar. The sky turned white.

'He put a detonator inside the wall,' Captain Valiant shouted. 'I should have guessed the house was boobytra—'

That was when the blast hit us.

CHAPTER 7

Captain Valiant held me against his chest as energy crackled and sparked across his back. My skin tingled and I felt dizzy. I heard a grunt and a groan, then Captain Valiant went limp. Whatever had exploded in Mr Kirby's attic, it had knocked him out.

I grabbed his arms. He was a lot heavier than I expected; those bacon sandwiches had piled on too many pounds. I strained every muscle but I couldn't hold him.

Captain Valiant plummeted to the ground. He'd taken the full force of the blast and now he was going to take the full force of the landing. I looked

down and saw what was left of Mr Kirby's house. It had been blown apart. Steam and smoke covered everything.

There was nothing I could do. Captain Valiant

crashed through wood and metal and glass. I winced as he hit the ground. It may have been my imagination, but I was sure he didn't hit it as hard as he should have. It was as if something had slowed him down.

But I didn't have time to find out if I was right. I heard a laugh that was far too loud and far too deep. It came from across the road where an old man stood on the pavement. I knew who the man was. There was no mistaking the bald head, glasses, brown jacket and grey trousers.

'Mr Kirby,' I said to myself.

By now, people were coming out of their homes to find out what had happened. Women held the hands of children, men talked in groups, teenagers took pictures with mobile phones. None of them knew the danger they were in. They couldn't see Captain Valiant lying in the rubble.

'Don't do anything stupid, Kirby!' I shouted. 'It'll be easier if you give yourself up!'

Mr Kirby laughed again. The laugh seemed to

shake his whole body. He fell to his knees and glared at me. His eyes flashed bright yellow. His face twisted and his cheeks bulged.

'I've already done what I had to do,' he said. 'I only wish my brother was here to see this. He thought he was the clever one.' He held out his hands. His fingers stretched into long, sharp claws. 'The school was only meant to be a test, but this . . . this is more than either of us imagined. Who wants to rule the world when you can remake it? It's alive, Dynamic Boy. I don't know what it is and I don't know how it found me, but it's alive. It's alive!'

Mr Kirby's head swelled like a balloon. His legs and arms stretched. His clothes ripped like paper and his skin sprouted thick, black fur. It was like watching someone turn into a gorilla; except this gorilla was twice the height of a man, had long horns and glistening fangs.

'I am Abaddon the Destroyer,' he roared. 'I am the beginning and the end of all things. Surrender to me now, Dynamic Boy, or prepare to meet your doom!'

Abaddon leapt towards me. It was an impressive leap. He went from one side of the road to the other. It was a pity he didn't let the smoke clear before he jumped. He crashed into the ruins of Mr Kirby's house, went head over heels, slid across the floor and thudded into a bath. He scrambled to his feet, punching and kicking everything out of his way.

Abaddon roared a second time. Glass rattled and plaster cracked. He looked as if he was about to leap at me again when a toilet suddenly rose into the air and crashed down on his head.

Abaddon fell on his face and lay still.

'Good shot,' I said. 'But Mum's going to be furious with you.'

Moon Girl removed the hood of her cloak. She knelt next to Captain Valiant.

'Dad's more important than Mum at the moment,' she said. 'I tried to catch him but he fell too quickly. My mind couldn't hold on. I managed to slow him down but I don't think it was enough.'

I pointed towards a big, green ball in the sky. 'Mum's left the particle web open. I know you can lift yourself up there, but can you manage Dad as well?'

'I've told you before,' Moon Girl said, 'it's not the weight of an object that's the problem. It's the shape and size. My mind has to get a good grip, that's all.' She glanced at the people who stood on the street. Some had been sensible enough to run away. Others came closer to get a look at Abaddon. 'What about them?' she asked.

'They'll have to look after themselves. We need to get Dad home and tell Mum what's happened. Ms Victory is the only one who can help us now.'

CHAPTER 8

I was right. Mum was furious. When she found out Emma had turned invisible and sneaked through the particle web, she gave us the usual lecture about not using our powers in the house. But I had the feeling she wasn't angry at Emma or me, she was worried about Dad. We all were. Even when Mum shouted she looked at the containment chamber where Dad hovered. A particle web moved around him.

'I'm sorry,' Emma said. 'I was only trying to help.'

'If your father had needed help, he would have asked for it.'

'But she saved Dad's life,' I said. 'Emma was the only one who could have got him back through the particle web. Abaddon might have killed him.'

Mum put her hand on the containment chamber as if she could touch Dad through the glass.

'I know,' she said. 'And I can't tell you how glad I am that she sneaked through the web. It's just . . . if what you've told me about Abaddon is true, then we've a lot more to worry about than your father's injuries.' Mum sat at a computer and started typing. The keyboard rattled against the table. 'What really bothers me is what happened to Mr Kirby. Now, are you sure he said, "it's alive"?'

Emma groaned. 'You're going to get all scientific, aren't you?' she said. 'I hate it when you get all scientific.'

Mum sighed. 'No, I'm not going to get all

scientific. But if you paid a bit more attention when I did get all scientific, you might understand why I've just sent out a planetary alert.'

'A planetary alert!' I said. 'But that means the Astral Knights are on their way! We don't need them. We can deal with this on our own!'

'No, we can't, Mark. This creature called Abaddon . . . he isn't what he appears to be.'

Emma sat on a chair and folded her arms. 'He's a big, hairy monster with horns and fangs,' she muttered.

'Actually, he's a transmorphic energy anomaly,' Mum said.

'You see, you're getting all scientific. That's it, I'm not listening any more.' Emma put her hands over her ears.

'What's a transmorphic energy thingy?' I asked.

'It's something very dangerous and very unstable,' Mum replied. 'When I examined the microwave your father found, I discovered some strange energy patterns. It took me a while to work out what they were, but now I'm certain.'

'I don't care what you're saying,' Emma said, 'I'm not listening.'

Mum ignored her. 'You see, when that microwave blew a hole in space, it also ripped a hole in time. It allowed a form of energy to leak from the past into the present; and it's that energy which has turned Mr Kirby into Abaddon.'

'But it can't be energy,' I said. 'Energy doesn't live; and Mr Kirby said it was alive.'

'Mark, you don't need to be made of skin and bone to be alive.' As she spoke, Mum typed so fast that her fingers became a blur. 'That's why I've sent out a planetary alert. The Astral Knights have experience of these kinds of things. Abaddon is far too dangerous. If that energy came into contact with one of us . . .' She looked up at Dad. 'You don't know how lucky your father is. He only has a few broken bones. If he'd been any closer to the explosion, I hate to think what might have happened. Now, why don't you and Emma go upstairs? I need to sort a few things out. When I'm finished, I'll come up.'

I could tell Mum didn't want to say any more. I pulled Emma out of her chair as I left.

'I'm still not listening,' she said.

Upstairs in the kitchen, we sat at the table. It was strange, sitting there in our costumes. Usually, when we were in the kitchen, we were like a normal family. We ate our meals, laughed and argued just like everyone else. After all, you can't be a superhero when you're pouring milk on your cornflakes or dripping spaghetti down your chin.

'I don't care what Mum thinks,' Emma said. 'I don't want the Astral Knights here. If we can't beat Abaddon ourselves, they'll think we can't do our jobs properly. And you know what that means.'

Yes, I did. This was our first assignment as Astral Guardians. If the Astral Knights reported back to Astral Command that we'd messed up, we'd be dismissed or sent back into training. Either way, we'd have to leave the Earth.

'I like it here,' Emma said. 'Don't you?'

'Of course I do,' I replied. 'But this isn't about what we like or dislike. It's about whether we  can do our jobs properly. The Astral Knights will do whatever they think is right. Just because we like it here won't make a difference to them.'

'Which is why we have to sort this out on our own. I'm not going to sit and wait for the Astral Knights to boss me around!'

The doorbell rang. Emma jumped out of her chair, threw her hood over her head and disappeared.

'Well, that's great,' I said. 'Tell you what, if it's the Astral Knights, I'll let them know you're out saving the world all by yourself. They'll be sooo impressed!'

CHAPTER 9

Emma needn't have worried. It wasn't the Astral Knights — it was David. From the look of him, I guessed he hadn't been home. I suppose he'd wandered around trying to find something to do. As I opened the door, I hid my costume with a simple illusion: jeans and a sweatshirt. I needn't have bothered.

'It was massive,' David said, running into the house without looking at me. 'It was big and furry with claws and teeth. It smashed through the school gates and ripped them out of the ground.'

I was wrong. David hadn't tried to find something to do. Something had found him.

'It picked up people and threw them around. Everyone was screaming and shouting. Then it ran up to the hole and jumped in. I don't know why, it just did; and Mr Stephenson . . . well, it grabbed Mr Stephenson. It smashed open the gates, grabbed Mr Stephenson and jumped in the hole. Then rocks started to fly. They landed everywhere. I saw this woman push her children inside a car and then . . .

. . . right through the roof!'

David took a deep breath.

'I thought . . .' he said, gazing round as if he didn't know where he was, 'I thought I might be able to find Captain Valiant. If he knew what was going on, he'd stop it.'

I led David into the living room and sat him on the sofa.

'I came here because there was no one at home . . . no one who . . .' David's lips trembled. I thought he was going to cry. 'Do you know where Captain Valiant is, Mark?'

Even though he spoke to me, David didn't look at me. His eyes were wide and staring, like a doll's eyes. He started to shiver. I put my hand on his forehead. He was hot and sweaty.

'Don't you dare,' Emma said. 'We're in enough trouble already.'

An invisible hand grabbed my arm.

'He's in shock,' I said. 'He needs my help.'

I pulled my arm away. Emma might have been older than me but that didn't mean she could tell me what to do.

'But you know how dangerous it is, Mark. Dad always told you not to put illusions inside people's heads. You can mess with their eyes but you can't mess with their minds.'

'Well, Dad's not here now.' I tried to sound confident. 'Don't worry. I know what I'm doing.'

It was true, I did know what I was doing. I just  didn't know what would happen after I'd done it. I kept my hand on David's forehead and concentrated. If he was looking for Captain Valiant then I'd let him find Captain Valiant in the one place where it was safe to find a superhero: in his imagination. David's eyes flickered and closed. I eased him back on the sofa.

'He'll be all right here,' I said. 'Mum's in the laboratory and by the time she comes up we'll be in more than enough trouble. It won't take her long to work out where we've gone.'

Emma took off her hood and glared at me. 'Where are we going?' she asked.

'To school, of course. That's where Abaddon is and that's where we need to be.' I made my costume reappear. 'You heard what David said. Abaddon is attacking innocent people. He probably went to the school looking for the microwave. When he finds it's not there . . . well, you said you didn't want to wait until the Astral Knights arrived.'

'I say a lot of things but that doesn't mean I want you to listen.' Emma nodded at David. 'What about him? Are you sure the illusion you've put inside his head won't do any harm?'

'It shouldn't. For the next few hours he'll lie there dreaming about Captain Valiant. By the time he wakes up, it'll all be over.'

'It might be over for us if this goes wrong.'

I shrugged. 'If we get it wrong then the Astral Knights will have to sort it out. And if that's the case, then it's goodbye Captain Valiant, Ms Victory, Moon Girl and Dynamic Boy. David will have to dream about other superheroes in silly costumes.'

'I like my costume,' Emma said.

'Of course you like it. You have a cloak of invisibility. I'd like my costume if I didn't have to look at it.'

CHAPTER 10

Even though Emma could use her powers to lift herself, she couldn't fly like me or Dad. I had to carry her on my back. When we landed outside the school gates, I groaned as she climbed off.

'I'm not that heavy,' Emma said.

'You're not that light either,' I replied.

The road was empty and quiet. A number of cars had been abandoned. One sat with its engine running and its doors open. A radio crackled with static. All the houses seemed deserted. It was obvious why: there were huge rocks everywhere. Roofs were smashed and windows broken. It looked as if it had been raining stone.

David was right about the gates. One of them lay on the grass. The other was stuck in the mud near the hole. Moon Girl and I walked through the gap where the gates had been, squelching across the grass.

'It's too quiet,' Moon Girl said. 'When it's this quiet, you know there's going to be trouble.'

'Then keep talking,' I said.

We got as close to the hole as we could. It had steep sides and a flat base.

At the bottom was a tunnel. The entrance was large, round and dark. It looked too round to be natural.

'Well, that explains where all the rocks came from,' Emma said.

'But it doesn't explain what happened to him.'

I pointed into the hole. There was a body near the tunnel. Even though it didn't have a head, I knew it belonged to Mr Stephenson. I could tell by the socks. Mr Stephenson always wore bright red socks. As we stared at the body, a rumbling drone came from inside the tunnel. The ground shook.

'What's that?' Moon Girl asked.

'I don't know. But I don't think we should wait around long enough to find out.'

But we *had* waited around long enough to find out. The cause of the drone shot out of the tunnel in thick, glistening, white coils which twisted and knotted themselves around each other. It looked like a giant worm, only it had Mr Stephenson's head. Lots of people said Mr Stephenson had a big head; well now he had a massive one.

'Move,' I shouted, pushing Moon Girl out of the way.

The worm dived between us, biting into the grass. It rose up chewing mud and stone. Mr Stephenson looked at me, hissed and spat. I flew away just in time. His teeth snapped at the air under my feet.

'The gates,' I shouted, hoping Moon Girl could hear me. 'Use the gates!'

A slimy coil wrapped itself around my legs. I tried to get away but the worm was too strong. Mr Stephenson's head grinned.

'The gates!' I shouted again.

This time I saw the teeth coming. Long, white fangs dripping with yellow saliva slashed at my body. I dodged them by letting the coils drag me towards the hole; but I knew I wouldn't be so lucky next time. If Moon Girl didn't do something quickly . . .

I heard a whistle and a

WHOOSH

A black blur spun above my head and cut through the worm's coils, slicing off Mr Stephenson's head. White gunge spurted into the air. The coils thrashed about, spattering gunge everywhere.

I felt the worm's grip weaken and I pulled myself free. I flew down to stand on the edge of the hole again.

'I feel sick,' Moon Girl said as she removed the hood of her cloak. 'Don't worry,' I said. 'If you throw up, no one will notice the mess.' The coils of the worm

writhed and twitched.
Mr Stephenson's head
rolled down the side of the
hole and disappeared under
them. A spinning gate hovered
over the worm's body before
dropping with a splat.

'What do we do now?' Moon Girl asked.

The worm's body gave one final jerk and
stopped moving.

'We have to find Abaddon,' I replied. 'You
remember what Mum said about Mr Kirby being
infected with a kind of energy? Well, maybe
Abaddon did this to Mr Stephenson; and if he
turned Mr Stephenson into that,' I pointed at the
worm, 'imagine what he could do to other people.'

'I am,' Emma said. 'That's why I want to go
home.'

Behind the school, a plume of smoke curled
into the sky. It was thick and black and looked as
if someone had scribbled on the clouds with a
marker.

'We can't go home,' I said, staring at the smoke. 'We have to find out what that is. After what's happened here, I have a feeling it's something to do with Abaddon.'

CHAPTER 11

The smoke came from the shops on the High Street. Moon Girl and I landed on the roof of the post office. It was one of the oldest buildings in town. There were spires at the four corners and a big, arched entrance. It was a bit like Dracula's castle. From the roof we could see along the High Street in both directions. It was a mess.

I could taste the fire in the air. There were crashed cars along the pavement; some of them had driven into shop windows. A set of traffic lights lay on the bonnet of a Range Rover. The traffic lights flashed red, amber and green over and over again.

A bus stood in the middle of the road. Its roof had been torn off and its seats ripped up. I saw handbags and coats in the twisted metal. Everywhere I looked there were signs of people: an overturned wheelchair, a bag of shopping dropped on the ground, a shoe, a scarf, a half-eaten burger; but there was no one to be seen. The only thing that moved along the High Street was smoke.

'What happened here?' Moon Girl asked.

I was about to reply when the bus in the middle of the road screeched. It slid across the tarmac as a red blob oozed from under it. The blob had

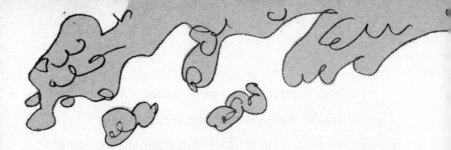

long, red tentacles. They wriggled up the sides of the bus and squirmed over the mangled seats. At the end of each tentacle was a person's head. Each head chewed on anything it could find, spitting out whatever it couldn't swallow.

'That's what happened,' I said. 'Abaddon's been here. He's infected everything with his energy.'

'But why?'

'I don't know. Maybe he can't help himself. Maybe he's like a virus that spreads from person to person. Or maybe he's just very, very nasty.'

Moon Girl grabbed my arm. 'We should wait for the Astral Knights,' she said. 'We can't fight this. What if we get infected?'

From across the street, I heard the crash of glass. A man kicked his way through a shop window. His clothes were torn and dirty. His face was stained with smoke. He coughed and fell on to the pavement. The blob also heard the breaking glass.

Every head turned to look at the man. They opened their mouths and bared their teeth.

Before we could do anything, the tentacles attacked the man. They bit into his arms and legs and dragged him across the road, pulling him under the bus. The man screamed, but not for long. When the tentacles reappeared, every head was licking its lips.

'I want to go now,' Moon Girl said. 'Mum was

right. We should wait for the Astral Knights.'

Yes, Mum was right. But when I looked along the High Street, I saw something which frightened me more than the tentacles and the heads. Running down the middle of the road, heading straight for the blob, was a boy in a mask and cape. The mask looked as if it was made from a duster. The cape looked as if it was made from a curtain.

'Never fear,' the boy shouted. 'I am here. Captain Valiant will save the day!'

Moon Girl and I both knew who it was: we recognised the voice. It was David.

CHAPTER 12

'How did he get here?' Moon Girl said. 'And why is he wearing one of our living room curtains?' She punched me. 'I told you not to put an illusion inside his head. Now he thinks he's Captain Valiant.'

I looked at the blob. All the heads opened their mouths and bared their teeth again.

'I have no idea how he got here,' I said. 'Maybe he walked. Maybe he ran. Maybe he flew. All I

know is that he's about to get himself eaten and it's all my fault. I have to do something to help him!' I leapt off the roof before Emma could stop me.

I got to David at the same time as the first tentacle. A head went to bite his leg. I stamped the head into the pavement with a crunch. I pulled David into the air and tried to fly back to the post office.

David may have been small but he wasn't light.

He didn't seem to understand what I was doing. He struggled in my grip, throwing punches at the tentacles. He even made noises with each punch.

'Bash, bang, pow!' he shouted. 'Come on, you can't beat me. I'm Captain Valiant!'

'Oh no, you're not,' I said. 'You're a schoolboy wearing a duster and a curtain.'

A car whizzed past my head and crashed into the blob.
Moon Girl!
Even at this
distance her
ability to
move objects
with her

mind came in handy; although her aim was a bit off. The car only just missed me.

The tentacles now lost interest in David. One by one, they looked up and saw Moon Girl on the roof. Two of them snaked towards her. They didn't get far – she gripped them with her thoughts and tied them in a knot!

The blob squealed. The bus it was hidden under shot into the air and soared over the post office. Moon Girl caught the bus before it crashed down on top of her. She hurled it back; but the blob was clever. A tentacle came up from the far side of the roof. Moon Girl saw it in time and dodged out of the way as a head sank its teeth into her cloak. But more and more tentacles slid up the walls, and attacked her from all sides.

I flew as fast as I could. David was still punching and kicking the air and I almost dropped him. When I reached her, Moon Girl was surrounded. She kept the tentacles back by wrapping them around each other, but they started biting and tearing at the roof. It wouldn't be long before she fell through; and if she was knocked out, that was it, she wouldn't be able to fight them off any more.

I didn't know what to do. Moon Girl needed my help. David needed my help. There were too many tentacles to fool them all with an illusion. I wasn't super-strong or super-fast. I couldn't move objects with my mind. I was super-useless. My sister was about to get eaten by a giant, red blob and my friend thought he was a superhero. Why hadn't I listened to Mum and waited for the Astral Knights?

A tentacle appeared in front of me. The head snarled, opened its mouth and gnashed its teeth. I dropped David, fell on to the roof and put my hands up to protect myself.

But the head exploded. It burst into green
flame and disappeared in a puff of smoke. All that
remained was a red, smouldering stump which
flopped around like a stranded fish. The other
tentacles stopped attacking Moon Girl. Every head
looked at me and at the green flame which
flickered over my fingers.

A green flame! I couldn't believe it!

I lifted my hands again and fire shot from my
palms, burning the tentacles. Every head exploded.
Some tried to get away but the green flame chased
them, flowing over the roof and down the walls.
The blob squealed as the fire swept across the road.
There was a loud bang, like a balloon bursting, and
the air was filled with red goo.

I glanced at Moon Girl. She looked as surprised as me.

'It's the gamma flame,' she said.

'I know,' I replied.

David leapt about the roof punching the air. 'No one beats Captain Valiant,' he said. 'I am invincible.'

Moon Girl pointed at my hands. 'But it's the gamma flame,' she said. 'You have the gamma flame.'

'Yes, he does,' a man replied. 'And that's why you're coming with us. The gamma flame should only be used by an Astral Knight.'

Moon Girl and I turned round. A man in a black uniform with a silver star on his shoulder stood on the opposite side of the roof. As quickly as the green flame had appeared, it vanished.

David saw the man, went up to him, stuck his chest out and said, 'I am Captain Valiant.'

The man was not impressed. 'Is that anything to do with you?' he asked as David ran round the roof.

'Yes, sir,' I replied. 'I put an illusion inside his head. I didn't think . . . I was only trying to . . .'

The man took a deep breath and frowned. 'Then it's a good job we've arrived,' he said. 'You two seem to have forgotten what it means to follow orders.'

CHAPTER 13

So they were here: the Astral Knights. I shouldn't have been surprised. When Mum sent out a planetary alert there was bound to be someone monitoring our sector of the galaxy. After all, the Astral Knights didn't take tea breaks or holidays. Some said they didn't even sleep.

They'd sent a star cruiser, one of the most powerful ships in the fleet. Whenever the Astral Knights responded to a planetary alert, they always

sent the biggest and best ships. As soon as we were
on board, Dad was taken to the medical unit.
Mum, Emma and I were taken to the crew
quarters. David went to have his mind cleaned up
– I don't know where they took him. I asked, but
no one would tell me anything.

The star cruiser was a typical military ship.
There were lots of long, dark corridors where
people walked in silence. There were lots of signs

which said, *No Entry* or *Authorised Personnel Only*.
The only lights were pale, white discs set into the
walls and ceilings. Everyone wore the same black
uniform with a silver star on the shoulder.

That's what it was like in the Astral Knights. No
one needed a silly costume to do their job.
Everyone knew what was expected and everyone
followed orders.

'Why should Mark have the gamma flame?'
Emma said. 'I'm the oldest. I've also got better
powers. All he can do is create illusions and fly. I've
seen magicians do better tricks than that.'

We sat in a small, circular room. It was the kind
of room designed to make people feel
uncomfortable. There were two benches facing
each other with a table between them. We were
still dressed in our superhero costumes. I'd never
felt so silly. The three of us looked like we'd turned
up for a fancy dress party that had been cancelled.
I stared at my hands.

'I don't think it is the gamma flame,' I said. 'It
can't be. The gamma flame is the most destructive

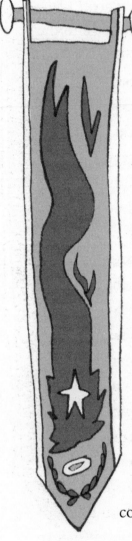

power in the universe. Only the Astral Knights are allowed to use it. No one gets it by accident.'

Mum shook her head. 'You're wrong, Mark. It *was* the gamma flame. And you're also wrong about it being a destructive power. The gamma flame is a creative power. It's what made the Big Bang go bang.'

Emma huffed and folded her arms. 'Here we go again,' she said. 'You're going to get all scientific. Why does everything have to be so complicated?'

'Emma,' Mum snapped, 'you've just fought three transmorphic energy anomalies and now you're sitting in a star cruiser orbiting the Earth. Which bit of that isn't complicated?'

'The bit where he gets the gamma

flame and I get attacked by a giant red blob!'

'It's not the gamma flame!' I shouted. 'It's . . . well, I don't know what it is. But it can't be the gamma flame. I'm not an Astral Knight!' I held up my hands. 'I don't want the power to blow up planets. I'm not old enough.'

Mum sat next to me and put her arm round my shoulder. 'You're not going to blow up planets,' she said, kissing my head. 'This isn't your fault, Mark. If you want to blame anyone for what's happened then blame the Black Phantom and his brother. Do you remember those strange energy readings I told you about – the energy which turned Mr Kirby into Abaddon? Well, when you and your father were caught in that explosion, I think you came into contact with this energy.'

'Oh great,' Emma muttered. 'Now he's going to turn into a monster.'

'No, he's not going to turn into a monster,' Mum said. 'The energy doesn't affect us in the same way it affects humans. We're protected. When we were given our powers by Astral Command we had a little bit of the gamma flame put inside us. The gamma flame is what makes us superheroes. Normally, it's under control. But this energy has let it loose.'

Emma shot out of her seat. 'So I might be able to use it as well. I was there when Mr Kirby's house exploded.' Emma stuck her hands out and waved them around. 'Do I have to say something?'

'It doesn't work like that,' Mum said. 'Mark was very stressed. He wasn't thinking about what he was doing.'

'That's because he doesn't have a brain.' Emma gritted her teeth. 'If I concentrate hard enough,

I'm sure I can ... wait, something's happening. Yes,
I can feel it, something's definitely happening!'

A tiny ball of green fire shot out
of Emma's backside and flew
across the room.

'I hope that doesn't
smell as bad as it looks,'
I said.

The fire bounced off
the walls, spiralled over our heads and
landed in the palm of a man who was
standing in the doorway. The man
laughed.

'I'm sorry,' he said. 'I couldn't resist a
little joke.'

The fire dissolved in the man's hand as
he walked into the room. He was short and
stocky with a bald head. I didn't recognise
him, but there was something about his

manner which made Mum and I stand up. The
man looked at each of us in turn.

'My name is Captain Zarax,' he said with a
grim smile. 'I am in charge of this ship and, as of
now, I am your superior officer.' The smile
broadened. 'You will be pleased to know that
Astral Command has placed you under my
authority.'

CHAPTER 14

There was only one light in the room. It was large and round and sat in the middle of the ceiling. As Captain Zarax spoke to us, the light gleamed off his head.

'On Earth, they call you "superheroes", don't they?' he said. 'How very colourful. I suppose you have a team name.' He stood in front of me. 'Let me guess: the Unbelievables.' He stood in front of Emma. 'Or is it the Unforgettables?' He stood in front of Mum. 'How about the I-Don't-Know-How-To-Follow-Orders-ables?'

'That's ever such a lot of balls, sir,' I said.

Captain Zarax turned to me. The light shone off his head so brightly I squinted.

'You're Dynamic Boy, the one who used the gamma flame.' He lifted his hand. The tip of his forefinger burnt with green fire. 'Impressive, isn't it? Do you know how long it takes an Astral Knight to learn how to use the gamma flame?'

'Long enough to know that it's not a good idea to play practical jokes, sir.'

Captain Zarax didn't find this funny. His eyes narrowed and he leant closer. 'Long enough to know when to speak and when to keep quiet.' He poked me in the chest with his burning finger. 'This isn't like any power you've ever known, boy. It could melt your brain in an instant and not leave a mark.'

'Then it's probably not a good idea to pick your nose, sir.'

'Mark, that's enough!' Mum pulled me to her side. 'I'm sorry, Captain Zarax. He doesn't mean to be rude.'

'Oh yes, he does,' Emma said.

Captain Zarax turned to face her. 'What a lovely daughter you have, Ms Victory. You must be so proud.'

'She has her moments,' Mum replied.

Captain Zarax held his burning finger under Emma's nose. 'There's no need to be jealous of your brother,' he said. 'Power isn't what you think it is. The gamma flame doesn't make you brave. It merely makes you dangerous.'

'Who cares about being brave,' Emma said. 'I just like the colour green.'

Captain Zarax blew out the flame. 'Then you've learnt nothing from what happened today. Astral Command was right. It's obvious you don't know what you're dealing with; but there again, real power is not something an Astral Guardian can be expected to understand. You have a simple job: protect the Earth from human and alien threats. Unfortunately, this threat isn't alien or human.'

Captain Zarax put his hands behind his back and rocked on his feet.

'That's why I have orders to do whatever is necessary to cleanse the Earth.' He lowered his voice. 'I'm sure at least one of you knows what that means.'

It seemed Mum did. She sat down and put her head in her hands.

'Of course,' Captain Zarax went on, 'there will be no need to destroy the planet, just the people, animals and plants. Naturally, none of this would be necessary if Abaddon had been dealt with properly: a direct hit by the gamma flame would have been  enough. However, Abaddon is still alive and the energy inside him is still spreading, so I have no choice.'

'Of course you have a choice,' I said. 'Why don't you destroy Abaddon yourself? You can use the gamma flame.'

Captain Zarax held my gaze. His eyes didn't blink as he spoke. 'What you fail to understand, Dynamic Boy, is that the energy which created Abaddon is pure chaos. It shouldn't be here. It will undo millions of years of evolution. It will deform and distort every form of life. The Earth, as you know it, will die a slow, horrible death.'

'But that doesn't explain why you won't destroy Abaddon,' I said. 'If he's so dangerous, send someone down there to get rid of him! I'll do it myself if you show me how!'

Mum's hand took hold of mine. 'It's too risky, Mark,' she said. 'The gamma flame might protect you and the Astral Knights from being infected but it won't protect you from Abaddon or the monsters he's created. Captain Zarax can't risk his crew for the sake of one planet.'

'But it's not just one planet. It's our home!'

'The only home you have is where Astral Command sends you,' Captain Zarax said. 'What you think or feel about the Earth is unimportant. This situation has to be dealt with quickly. To be honest, I don't think Astral Command cares how it's done. A small team may be successful but a gamma blast is the only way to be certain that Abaddon is destroyed and the energy neutralised.' He stared at me. 'It's ironic, really. This whole thing started with a hole in time. If only you'd known what to do with the gamma flame when you had time, Dynamic Boy, you might have saved the Earth. But you didn't and now I have to make up for your mistake.'

A ball of green fire flew from his hand and hovered over our heads.

'Follow this,' he said. 'It will take you to Captain Valiant. He is fully recovered and you will want to discuss what to do now that your assignment on Earth is over. I'm sure you can think of a way of explaining to Astral Command why you failed to do your jobs.' Captain Zarax stared at the green ball as if looking at something inside it. 'But so I can be sure there is no misunderstanding between us, I want you to know, Ms Victory, that I have been made aware of your particular skills.' He paused. 'I hope this will not be a problem.'

Mum stood up. 'No, sir,' she said.

'Then I hope you understand what is expected of you. As I said, a small team might be successful but it would be risky and, as I'm sure you know, risks should only be taken by those with the skills to take them.'

Mum glanced at me. I'd never seen her look so worried.

'Yes, sir,' she said. 'I understand.'

CHAPTER 15

We followed the green ball along lots of dark corridors until we came to the medical unit. We met no one along the way. When we reached the medical unit, the green ball vanished. As soon as we were inside, the door slid shut behind us.

Dad sat on a bed which looked as uncomfortable as the benches in the crew quarters. You would have thought a medical unit would have been built to make people feel better. Apart from a few lights in the walls, it was as gloomy as the rest of the ship.

Mum went over to Dad and put her arms around him. It was one of those parent moments. Emma and I looked away.

'How are you two?' Dad asked as soon as Mum let go.

Emma shrugged. I grunted.

'So you're both all right?'

I shrugged. Emma grunted.

Mum whispered in Dad's ear. The two of them started talking in low voices, the way parents do when they don't want children to hear what they're saying.

Emma muttered something under her breath. She held up her hands and flexed her fingers. I knew what she was trying to do.

'Maybe you weren't close enough to the explosion,' I said. 'Dad and I got a direct hit.'

'I was close enough to that red blob,' she replied. 'Something must have happened.' She glared at her palms. 'Fire up!'

Nothing happened.

'Emma, I don't think a catchphrase is going to work.'

'It might. I just have to find the right one.' Emma dropped one arm, stuck the other up in the air and closed her eyes. 'Go, gamma, go!'

I shook my head.

'This is ridiculous. All life on Earth is about to be destroyed and you're practising to be a cheerleader.'

'Then why don't you do something about it, Dimwit Boy!' Emma kicked me. 'Oh, look at me, Captain Zarax, I can pick my nose and melt my brain at the same time. Well, go ahead. We wouldn't notice the difference!'

'Emma, stop it,' Mum said.

'No, I won't. If it isn't bad enough that he has the gamma flame, he doesn't even know how to use it. What's the point of having great power if you don't know how to use it?'

'Well, you know what they say,' Dad said. 'With great power comes great confusion.' He got off his bed and gave Emma a hug. For some reason, I felt very guilty.

'But it's not my fault,' I said. 'If I knew how to use the gamma flame, I would.'

Mum started to speak, changed her mind and went to a wall panel. She pressed a series of buttons with a confidence which showed she knew what she was doing. There was a low hum and a particle web appeared in the middle of the room. Its glow turned all of us a sickly shade of green.

'I told you before, Mark,' Mum said, 'you don't have to blame yourself; and you also don't have to know how to use the gamma flame. As long as you let me inside your head, I can do the rest.' She turned to face us. 'You see . . . I used to be an Astral Knight.'

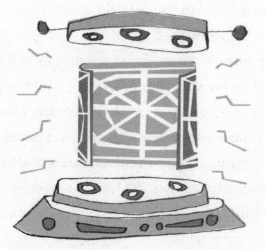

I don't know whose mouth dropped open the widest, mine or Emma's.

'The coordinates are set,' Mum said, pointing at the particle web, 'but I don't know how much time Captain Zarax will give us. We have to go now.'

'An Astral Knight?' Emma said. 'You can't be an Astral Knight. You're our mother.'

'I was a lot of things before I became your mother,' Mum said. 'And since it was a long time ago, I'd prefer not to talk about it. Sometimes the past should stay in the past. So, if you don't mind, we have a planet to save.'

'But won't Captain Zarax come after us?' I said.

'Don't you ever listen, Mark?' Mum replied. 'Captain Zarax may have his orders but I have to do what is expected of me. He has given us a second chance. We're the small team who has to take risks.' She smiled. 'I know it's been a while, but you don't forget how to use the gamma flame. It's like riding a bike.'

Dad put his hand on my shoulder and lowered his voice. 'Unfortunately,' he said, 'your mum can't ride a bike.'

CHAPTER 16

When I stepped out the other side of the particle web, I recognised where we were. It could only have been a few hours since I'd left. There was a Range Rover with a traffic light bent over its bonnet. There was a bus with its roof torn off. I saw handbags and coats, an overturned wheelchair and a bag of shopping.

In front of us was a building which looked like Dracula's castle. It was the post office. A black, oily mess dripped down its bricks. The black liquid spread across the pavement and formed a pool in the middle of the road. A head floated on the surface. It looked at me, grinned and sank with a gurgle.

'Did the gamma flame do this?' I asked.

'No,' Mum replied. 'Abaddon did this. Remember what Captain Zarax told you. The energy which turned Mr Kirby into Abaddon deforms and distorts all forms of life. The black liquid must be part of that process.'

'So it's a monster like the others,' Emma said.

'No. It's a transmorphic energy anomaly.'

Dad pulled Emma close. 'When a floating head grins at you,' he said, 'it doesn't matter what you call it.'

'Right, Mark,' Mum said, resting her hands on my neck, 'we have work to do. I want you to put an illusion inside my head. Now don't worry, you won't do to me what you did to David. All I need is a way into your mind. My Astral Knight training will do the rest. Just try to think of something which makes you happy.'

'Something
happy? I've
seen my
science
teacher
turned into a
monster, my
headmaster
turned into a
giant worm
and a head
floating in a
pool of black
gunge.'

'Then try to think of something which makes

you angry. I just need a strong emotion. What if I told you that Emma found a DVD under your bed last week, a DVD which you probably didn't want  me or your father to know about?' My hands burst into green flame. 'Good,' Mum said, 'that's more like it. Now, if I can just . . .'

The gamma flame shot across the road, shattering glass and smashing brick. The Range Rover with the traffic lights on its bonnet flipped over and crashed through a shop window.

'Oops,' Mum said, 'that wasn't quite what I planned. Still, I'm sure I'll get the hang of it eventually; besides, we need to get his attention.'

I was about to ask who she meant when something darted across the road near my feet. I thought it was a dog or a cat, but it was neither. It was a hand, running across the road on its fingers.

On the back of the hand was a pair of wings. The wings buzzed and the hand flew up. It circled over my head and dived towards me, its fingers clawing the air.

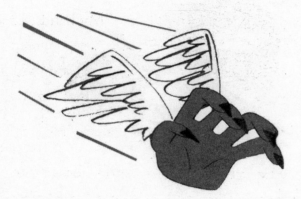

The gamma flame blasted the hand to bits. Smoking fingers and a burning thumb hurtled across the road, splashing into the black pool.

'That's disgusting,' Emma said.

'But at least it was armless,' Dad said, laughing at his own joke.

CHAPTER 17

Dad didn't laugh for long. More hands scuttled out of doorways and hopped through broken windows. It only took a few seconds before we were surrounded. The hands filled the air like flies.

Dad muttered something under his breath, tore off the doors of a car and flew into the swarm. Using the doors like bats, he squashed and crushed anything that got in his way. Bits of skin and bone fell everywhere. Whatever missed getting splattered by Dad was burnt by the gamma flame. Soon, the road was speckled with charred nails and smouldering knuckles.

Unfortunately, the hands weren't our only problem. There were arms as well. They wriggled out of drains and fell from gutters. If the hands were like flies then the arms were like maggots; only maggots with teeth. At every shoulder and elbow there was a mouth with snapping jaws.

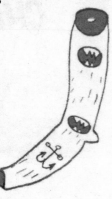

'Now this is really disgusting,' Emma said. She stared at the wriggling arms, and used her power to hurl them into the gamma flame.

They twisted and jerked before exploding with a **POP** and a

SIZZLE

'Get back, Emma!' Mum shouted. 'There are too many!'

Mum tried to aim the green fire at the arms. Instead, it roared across the street again, setting light to brick, metal and glass. Soon, the opposite side of the road was a wall of flame reaching up to the height of the buildings.

'I think I can do better on my own,' Emma said.

She grinned and stood with her legs apart, holding out her hands like a cowboy brandishing his guns. Wherever she pointed, an arm would fly

125

into the gamma flame. She even started to make gun noises.

'Bang! Pow!' she giggled. 'Forget Moon Girl. Make way for Cosmic Girl!'

More arms exploded and, as I watched, I felt more and more useless. The gamma flame may have been pouring from my hands but I wasn't doing anything. Mum was in control.

'I think I'll change my name to Doesn't-Do-Much Boy,' I muttered.

Thankfully, it didn't take long to swat, crush and burn everything that flew out of the shops or crawled along the street. Soon, there was nothing left except steaming blobs of pink mush and a sickly smell. The smell tickled the back of my throat and made me cough. When the last flying hand splashed on to the road and the last wriggling arm burst, Mum let go of me and the gamma flame vanished.

Dad landed beside us. He threw the car doors into the black pool. Together, he and Mum walked across the road, trying not to step in anything that bubbled or boiled. Emma blew on her fingers as if blowing smoke from the barrel of a gun. The smirk on her face really annoyed me.

'Have we beaten Abaddon?' I asked. 'Can we go home?'

Mum shook her head and pointed at the black pool. 'I don't think so,' she said. 'I have a feeling that what we're after is in there.'

The surface of the pool gurgled and churned. A wave of black gunge spilt across the street. The car

doors which Dad had thrown into the pool shot into the air and clanged against the post office wall.

'All right, *Cosmic* Girl,' I said, 'what are you going to do now?'

Emma pulled her hood over her head and disappeared.

I couldn't blame her. A head rose out of the pool. It had long, sharp horns, yellow eyes and white fangs. It looked like Abaddon, but it was different from the creature I'd seen at Mr Kirby's house. This thing was as tall as the post office and it had no body. Below the head was a column of swirling, black gunge. Within the gunge, I saw other heads, only these were human. They rolled around with wide, staring eyes and gaping mouths.

'Is that Abaddon?' I asked.

Mum and Dad backed away from the creature.

'It's what he has become,' Mum replied. 'I should have realised this would happen. Mr Kirby couldn't control the energy inside him. It was too powerful.'

Mum went to turn but lost her balance. Dad reached out to catch her but lost his balance as well. The reason was obvious. There was a black puddle around their feet and they were stuck in it. The black liquid had seeped through the cracks in the road. While we'd been staring at Abaddon, it had spread under us!

Emma screamed. I looked for her but couldn't see anything except an oily mess on the pavement. She screamed again.

'Mark!' Mum shouted. 'You have to use the gamma flame!'

CHAPTER 18

A second wave of black gunge spilt out of the pool and surged across the street. Dad saw the wave and did everything he could to get free, but the more he struggled the more he became stuck in the black liquid. Mum had the same problem. Both of them were glued to the road.

As for Emma, I saw concrete fly in all directions. She was also trying to get free. But it made no difference. Her invisible body was

being smothered in black gunge.

I raised my hands and glared at them as if they were to blame for what was happening. Where was the gamma flame? If only I could remember what I'd done when I was on the post office roof. Emma was right. What was the point in having great power if you didn't know how to use it?

It was then that my hands burst into flame. I almost swore. The gamma flame seemed to be playing games with me.

'Mark, look out!' Mum cried.

I didn't look out. I was too busy staring at my hands to notice the column of black gunge spurting up from the pavement. The gunge lifted the stone under my feet and sent me hurtling

through a shop window.
Thankfully, the window was already
broken. I went tumbling over wood
and glass to land face down in a pile
of women's underwear.
Why couldn't I have been
thrown through the window of a
sports shop? Sitting up, I pulled a
pair of knickers off my head.
A bra was wrapped under my arm
and around my neck. I tugged
at the strap.
'How do you get these things
off?' I groaned.
I tugged at the strap again. The
elastic snapped and smacked me in
the face. Rubbing my cheek, I stood
up and charged back into the street.
As I ran towards Mum and Dad,
the black gunge retreated in
front of me.
'He's scared of you!' Mum

shouted. 'Remember what Captain Zarax said. You can destroy Abaddon with a direct hit!' Mum pointed at the pool. 'A direct hit!'

I knew what she meant. Another column of gunge exploded from the ground, but this time it missed. I was already in the air, hands blazing, racing towards the black pool. There was only one way to make sure I got a direct hit and that was to plunge into the pool itself. I didn't want to. It made me sick to think of diving into that oily mess. But I had no choice. There was too much at stake. I had to trust Mum.

Abaddon seemed to know what I planned to do. Gunge erupted all around me. I had to dodge bricks and chunks of tarmac. As I dived into the pool, the black liquid tried to get away.

It opened up like a tunnel. The strange thing was, the tunnel didn't seem to end. I kept going down and down into a swirling darkness.

I stared at the tunnel walls. How was I supposed to get a direct hit now? I thought I might be able to touch the black liquid but, as I stretched out my hands, it moved away. And that wasn't all. There was something under the surface, just beyond my fingertips. They were faces; like the faint outlines of drawings which had been rubbed out. I guessed these must be the people Abaddon had infected. Somehow they were trapped inside the black gunge.

I hadn't expected this. I thought I would destroy Abaddon and that would be it. Now I had these people to think about. I had to find a way to help them. But how could I use the gamma flame to set them free and destroy Abaddon?

The answer was simple: I couldn't. The gamma flame was in control, not me. I didn't know what to do. I looked at the green fire.

'Why don't you do something useful and help these people?' I said.

The fire on my hands went out.

'No, that's not what I meant!' I cried. 'I need you. Don't let me down now!'

My body started to glow. My skin felt as if there were something crawling over it.

Green flames flickered through my costume, spreading from my head to my feet. I couldn't see clearly. The flames got bigger and the glow got brighter.

'What are you doing?' I shouted.

There was a

like the sound of wood snapping. I squinted through the green glare. The gamma flame had

burst through my chest, ripping me apart. I could feel my ribs splitting and splintering. I went to grab them, as if I could push them together and control the flames, but it was useless. The fire roared out of my body and exploded through the tunnel walls. I felt no pain. There was no heat; and yet I found myself in the middle of a green fireball which burnt everything it touched – including me!

CHAPTER 19

'Is he dead?'

I heard a voice but I couldn't see anything. Where was I?

'Emma, for the last time, he's not dead. The medical team have checked him over and he's fine. Now will you please go and help your mother.'

Was that Dad?

'Well, he looks dead to me. Maybe you should put his head in a bucket of water.'

'Don't you mean splash water on his face?'

'No. It would be much more fun to put his head in a bucket of water.'

I forced my eyes open. The light was too bright and it hurt. But the light wasn't green any more. And there was sky: a clear, blue sky. And my chest, it was in one piece. I could feel my ribs.

'Dad, is that you?' I croaked.

Captain Valiant looked down at me and smiled. 'Glad to have you back, Dynamic Boy. We've a lot of work to do and we need your help. I'm afraid you can't lie there taking it easy.'

Taking it easy? There was nothing easy about lying on a pile of bricks. Every edge and corner dug into my body. Captain Valiant helped me to my feet. I didn't feel much better when I stood up.

'What happened?' I said. 'Where's Abaddon?'

Captain Valiant patted me on the shoulder. I almost fell over.

'Abaddon's been destroyed,' he replied. 'You blew him up.'

'Yes, and made a right mess of it,' Moon Girl said.

She was right. I stood on the edge of a massive hole in the middle of the road. The street was only just recognisable as a street. Most of the shops didn't have fronts. There was shattered glass, broken wood and twisted metal everywhere. The post office was behind me. It still looked like Dracula's castle but now the walls were charred and blackened. Clouds of dust drifted along the pavement.

But that wasn't the worst of it. People wandered through the dust: men and women with confused expressions who didn't seem to know where they

143

were. They certainly didn't know they weren't wearing any clothes.

'I must admit, I didn't expect that,' Captain Zarax said. 'I knew the gamma flame would destroy Abaddon, but I didn't know it would remake the people he infected. That's the trouble with the gamma flame – sometimes it seems to have a mind of its own.'

He stood on the other side of the hole, surveying the street with a smile. It was as if he was proud of what he saw. As I listened to him, I had a horrible thought and looked down. I'd never been so happy to see my costume. The lightning flash on the front glistened in the sunlight.

Captain Zarax seemed to know what I was thinking.

'Don't worry, the gamma flame didn't remake you,' he said. 'You're its host. It may have been out of control for a while but that's taken care of now.' He tapped his forehead. 'While you were unconscious, my medical team repaired the blocks which kept it at bay. It's still inside you, just like it's inside the rest of your family, but that shouldn't be a problem. Unless, of course, you've decided to join the Astral Knights. From what I've seen, you'd make a good recruit.'

I shook my head. 'No, thank you. I'm happy to be an Astral Guardian. I've had enough of powers I don't understand. I'll stick with flying and creating illusions.'

Captain Valiant put his hands on his hips. 'We're a team,' he said. 'We wouldn't be complete without Dynamic Boy.'

'But at least I could have his room if he left home,' Moon Girl said. She then looked at the naked people. 'So whoever was infected by the energy has been put back together?' Captain Zarax sighed.

'I'm not in the habit of repeating myself, but yes, the people have been put back together. Of course, it may take their brains a while to make sense of everything, but they'll return to normal eventually. Why do you think your mother is assisting my crew to find . . . ah, here they are now.'

I hadn't noticed them before, but moving through the ruins of the street were Astral Knights. They helped people stand, stopped them falling over or sat them down to rest. Two now walked towards us, holding a naked man between them. The man looked like he was made of rubber. His whole body drooped.

'So that's Mr Kirby.' Captain Zarax squinted and frowned. 'I have to admit, for someone who almost destroyed the Earth, he's not very impressive. I expected him to be bigger. Still, after all the trouble he's caused, Astral Command has decided that he's coming with us. They don't want him to make any more gravity engines.'

The Astral Knights marched Mr Kirby to a particle web which glowed on the far side of the road. As they stepped into it, Mr Kirby started to burble and bawl like a baby. I wondered if he realised what was happening to him.

'And now that's done,' Captain Zarax said, 'our job here is complete; while yours,' he shaded his eyes from the sun and looked up, 'has only just started.'

In the distance I heard a soft, rhythmic thud. A line of black dots appeared on the horizon. They were probably helicopters; it was either the police or the army. They always turned up when the hard work was done.

'But at least it's a good job,' Ms Victory said, standing beside Captain Valiant. Her costume was smeared with dirt and there were smudges on her face. 'I've checked the buildings and there's no one trapped inside.' She winked at me. 'But it won't be long before everyone realises they're naked. Once that happens, they'll be running off in all directions. So we need everyone to think they're dressed. Do you think you can manage an illusion, Dynamic Boy?'

I nodded. 'No problem.'

'So whoever was infected by the energy has been put back together,' Moon Girl said again. She

climbed on to a pile of bricks and stared at the people as if looking for someone. 'Has anyone seen Mr Stephenson? And, more importantly, does anyone have a mobile phone? A few pictures of my headteacher without any clothes on might be very useful.' Moon Girl jumped off the bricks, pulled up her hood and disappeared.

'Don't you dare . . .' Ms Victory began, but she was talking to empty space. 'Moon Girl!' she called. 'You better not ignore me, young lady, because if you think . . .' Ms Victory dashed away.

'A good job?' Captain Zarax laughed to himself. 'That's not how I'd describe it. To be honest, I don't know how you cope, Captain Valiant. I couldn't stay on one planet when there's a whole universe to explore. It would be so boring.'

We'd just saved a planet and he was bored?! I'd hate to think what Captain Zarax found exciting.

'But this isn't just one planet, sir,' Captain Valiant replied. 'It's our home.'

'Yes, so I've been told.'

Captain Zarax scowled and walked away. He headed for the particle web along with the other Astral Knights. He didn't even look back as he stepped into the green glow and disappeared.

'That's the problem with the Astral Knights,' Captain Valiant said as the particle web also vanished. 'All that space to fly around in and nowhere to go.' He patted my shoulder again. 'Come on, let's get to work.'

'Right . . . yes . . . work . . .' I took a deep breath and tried to look like a superhero rather than a boy in a costume who ached from head to foot. For a moment, I stared at the spot where the particle web had been. Then I remembered something.

'Where's David?' I asked.

Captain Valiant went to speak but stopped himself. He scratched his head, pulled at his costume where it was tight around his stomach and coughed.

'David is safe,' he said at last. 'He's not here at the moment but he's definitely safe. We'll talk about him later.' He flew into the air. 'Right now we need an illusion to help these people. We need you to do what you're good at, Dynamic Boy!'

An illusion: it seemed that the only illusion Dad needed was the sort which stopped me asking questions. But he was right. We had to help these people; and since I was in control of my powers again, it was up to me. The gamma flame had done its job and now it was time to do mine. After all, Captain Valiant and me, Ms Victory and Moon Girl – we were superheroes. We had to save the world . . . even if we made a bit of a mess when we did it!

CAPTAIN VALIANT

And me

RETURN
OF THE
SILVER CYBORG

Algernon Pratt is the world's greatest computer
genius – and criminal mastermind.
His latest invention is a devious machine
that allows him to take over a person's mind –
and his first target is the man
who put him in prison:
Captain Valiant.

piccadillypress.co.uk/children

Go online to discover:

☆ more books you'll love

☆ competitions

☆ sneak peeks inside books

☆ fun activities and downloads